Rapunzel

Tangled

This edition published by Parragon in 2012
Parragon
Queen Street House
4 Queen Street
Bath BA1 1HE, UK
www.parragon.com

Adapted by: Irene Trimble
Edited by: Gemma Louise Lowe
Production by: Sarah Brown

Illustrated by: Jean-Paul Orpiñas, Studio IBOIX &
the Disney Storybook Artists.
Designed by: Pete Hampshire

ISBN 978-1-4454-9667-2

Printed in China

Rapunzel

Tangled

PaRragon

Bath · New York · Singapore · Hong Kong · Cologne · Delhi
Melbourne · Amsterdam · Johannesburg · Shenzhen

PROLOGUE

*O*nce upon a time, a single drop of sunlight fell from the heavens. From it, a magical flower bloomed that had the power to heal the sick and frail.

One day, an old woman named Mother Gothel discovered the Golden Flower whilst walking along a craggy hillside.

Just as she was about to pluck the flower, she noticed that it was glowing. As she sang, Mother Gothel's brittle voice became strong and clear, her old bones stopped aching and she was young again! Her eyes widened with selfish delight!

Mother Gothel decided to leave the flower

where it was, so that she alone could continue to covet its power.

Over time, a small but happy kingdom flourished nearby. Though the people of the kingdom had heard the legend of the Golden Flower, no one had ever seen it and, the truth was, they had never really needed the flower.

The Queen was to have a child, but all too soon, the kingdom's happiness came to an abrupt end, as the Queen became gravely ill. There seemed to be nothing that could help her.

Or was there? Perhaps the Golden Flower was more than merely an old legend.

Willing to try anything to save her, the people launched a search throughout the kingdom and all the surrounding lands.

Mother Gothel began to panic. My flower! she thought selfishly. They mustn't find it. It belongs to me!

"We found it! We found it!" exclaimed a guard.

Mother Gothel watched, horrified, as a palace guard uprooted the precious flower and carried it back to the castle.

The flower was made into a potion and fed to the ailing Queen. Its magic worked and the Queen recovered! The King and all the people in the land rejoiced.

Soon afterwards, the King and Queen stood on their royal balcony, holding the newborn princess. She was a darling baby, with her mother's emerald-green eyes, and curly golden hair that gleamed in the sunlight.

Meanwhile, without the magic of the Golden Flower, Mother Gothel was growing older by the day. Seething with anger, she waited.

As the day faded into night, the King and Queen launched a single glowing lantern into the night sky to celebrate their princess's birth.

The King and Queen's happiness was short-lived. For later that night, a vengeful Mother Gothel crept into the royal nursery and approached the Princess's cradle. The lovely golden curls of the infant entranced Mother

Gothel. Compelled to gently stroke the baby's hair, she quietly began to sing.

Most unexpectedly, the child's hair began to glow! Mother Gothel watched in shock, then delight, as her withered old hand became young again. The healing power of the Golden Flower lived on in the golden hair of the little princess!

Mother Gothel cut a piece of the princess's hair and gazed at it as it lay in her hand.

But that was not to be. Mother Gothel watched as the light hair in her hand turned dark brown. Mother Gothel realized that the magic only worked if she sang and stroked the hair on the princess's head!

There was only one thing to do. She would have to steal the baby… and keep her hidden from the rest of the world forever.

Chapter 1

$\mathscr{F}$or many years the people of the kingdom searched and searched, but they never found their princess. No one knew that far away, hidden in a boxed-in valley, Mother Gothel was raising the child as her own at the top of the tall tower they called home.

Mother Gothel adored Rapunzel and the child loved Mother Gothel too. After all, she was the only mother, and the only person, whom Rapunzel knew or remembered. She sang lullabies to the little girl as she stroked and brushed her hair every day.

Nearly four years passed before Rapunzel asked Mother Gothel, "Why can't I go outside?"

"The outside world is a dangerous place filled

with horrible, selfish people," she replied. She did not want to lose Rapunzel.

But on the night of her fourth birthday, Rapunzel tiptoed over to the tower window. There in the night sky she saw thousands of sparkling lights drifting up beyond the ridge of the valley towards the stars.

The same thing happened on the night of her fifth birthday, and on her sixth and seventh birthdays. Rapunzel loved those floating lights and she grew to believe that somehow they were meant for her.

Years passed, and Rapunzel grew into a beautiful young woman with sparkling green eyes and golden hair that was nearly seventy feet long. With her eighteenth birthday approaching, Rapunzel had decided that this birthday would be different. Mother Gothel had always told Rapunzel that someday, when she was old enough and ready, she would be allowed to go outside. Rapunzel nervously hoped that

Mother Gothel would finally allow her to go out, just once. She needed to find the source of those mysterious floating lights!

Opening the tower's shutters, Rapunzel leaned out over the windowsill, breathing in the fresh morning air. A tiny green chameleon named Pascal came out to greet her. Pascal was Rapunzel's only friend.

Pascal knew, as always, exactly what was best for Rapunzel. She wanted to go outside! But she couldn't go out – she needed Mother Gothel's permission.

Their day was about to begin – the day she would ask Mother Gothel to take her to see the sparkling lights!

Rapunzel kept herself busy every day. But today, Pascal felt her excitement as she rushed through her chores. Then she sat down to play her guitar. She was self-taught, of course, but the melodies that floated from the strings were beautiful.

Pascal tried to be patient as Rapunzel did the same things over and over again. This morning, when she was finally done with all her chores, her guitar, her puzzles and books, her hair.... Rapunzel smiled at Pascal. As usual, she had saved the best for last: painting! It was her passion. The tower's walls were covered with her art. Today, as she pulled back the red curtain that covered her favourite painting, she looked at it differently. She added a small picture of herself ready to enter the forest beyond the tunnel and see the world outside her little valley.

Suddenly, Rapunzel heard her mother's voice.

"Rapunzel!" Mother Gothel called from outside the tower. "Rapunzel! Let down your hair!"

Rapunzel gasped. The moment she had been waiting for had finally arrived!

"Okay," Rapunzel said to Pascal, trying to be calm. "No big deal, I'm just going to do it. I'm just going to say, 'Mother? There's something I've been wanting to ask you!'" She was beginning to feel her heart sinking. Maybe she wasn't ready to go outside.

Pascal took one look at Rapunzel and arched his little body, puffing out his chest to tell her to be brave.

Down below, Mother Gothel yelled, "Rapunzel! I'm not getting any younger down here!" Rapunzel hurried towards the window.

"Coming, Mother!" Rapunzel shouted. She placed a loop of her golden hair around a pulley outside the window and lowered it down.

Rapunzel began to pull Mother Gothel slowly up to the tower window. It was hard work!

"Hello, Mother!" Rapunzel said, nearly out of breath.

"Rapunzel, how do you manage to do that every day? It looks absolutely exhausting!"

"Oh, it's nothing," Rapunzel replied cheerfully.

"Then I don't know why it takes so long," Mother Gothel snapped, adding in the sweetest voice she could muster, "Oh, I'm just teasing."

"So… Mother?" Rapunzel began, stumbling nervously over her words. "As you know,

tomorrow I turn eighteen. And I wanted to ask… what I really want for this birthday… actually, I've wanted it for quite a few birthdays now…"

Mother Gothel shook her head impatiently.

"Oh, Rapunzel, please stop with the mumbling. You know how I feel about the mumbling. 'Blah blah blah!' It's very annoying."

Rapunzel sighed and then blurted out, "I want to see the floating lights!"

"What?" Mother Gothel said to Rapunzel.

"Well," Rapunzel answered, "I was hoping you would take me to see the floating lights this year."

"Oh, you mean the stars," Mother Gothel said.

Rapunzel shook her head. "That's the thing," she said excitedly. "I've charted stars and they're always constant. But these appear every year on my birthday and only on my birthday! And I can't help but feel that they're meant for me! I need to see them – in person. I have to know what they are."

"Go outside?" Mother Gothel said as she gathered her wits. "Why, Rapunzel, you know why we stay up in this tower."

"I know," Rapunzel replied. A shiver crept up her back as Mother Gothel described the terrible men, ruffians and thugs, and other frightening things in the outside world.

Mother Gothel kept going until she felt certain Rapunzel understood that she was responsible for protecting her gift. Then she spoke firmly:

"Rapunzel. Don't ever ask to leave this tower again."

"Yes, Mother," Rapunzel replied obediently.

Chapter 2

*A*t that very moment, a dashing thief named Flynn Rider and his partners in crime, the Stabbington brothers, were running through the forest as fast as they could. Hot on their heels were the highly-trained mounted palace guards. Flynn Rider and the Stabbington brothers, had stolen the crown that belonged to the long-lost princess.

Flynn Rider halted at a tree and tried to catch his breath. Noticing a WANTED poster of himself, he scoffed,

"Would you look at this?"

The Stabbington brothers stared blankly at the poster.

"Is it too much to ask to get my nose right?"

Flynn felt insulted. "It's just so… bulbous," he added, petulantly.

Though the burly Stabbington brothers were Flynn's partners for this one crime, they were probably the most dangerous cutthroats he had ever met and right now, he was worried that they might kill him for the crown. He needed a plan to escape them and the royal guards!

"Okay," Flynn said, thinking fast, "give me a boost and then I'll pull you up."

"Give us the satchel first," demanded the brother without the eye patch.

"What? I just can't believe that after all we've

been through together, you don't trust me!"

Grumbling, he handed the brothers the satchel containing the crown and began climbing over their shoulders. As he climbed, he grabbed the satchel back, unnoticed.

When he reached the top of the ledge, he held up the satchel and gave the brothers a grin.

"Enjoy prison!" he called back as he ran away.

The captain of the royal guard saw Flynn making a run for it.

"He's getting away!" he shouted.

The royal guards were hot on his trail, "Ha! We've got him now, Maximus!" the captain said to his muscle-bound white horse.

Grabbing a vine, Flynn swung through the air and looped back, knocking the captain right off his horse and taking his place in the saddle.

"Hee-yah!" Flynn yelled triumphantly, feeling pretty smug. He knew he'd pulled off a classic move. But his grin quickly left his face when the horse suddenly came to a halt, nearly throwing Flynn out of the saddle.

"Come on, Fleabag!" Flynn yelled.

Maximus was the best horse in the kingdom, and he did not like being called Fleabag. The horse whipped his head around angrily and started nipping at Flynn's precious satchel.

"Stop it! Stop it! Bad horse, bad horse!" Flynn shouted.

Maximus began spinning in circles, trying to throw Flynn off, but the young thief held on tightly.

"Whoa, who-o-o-o-oah!" Flynn shouted. He had a new enemy – a maniacal horse!

Man and horse engaged in a tug-of-war until Flynn used all his might to pull the satchel free, flinging it well out of reach on the end of a fallen tree that was rooted in the side of the cliff and stretched across the top of the deep ravine.

Flynn leaped from the horse's back and scrambled to get to the tree first. The horse walked out onto the tree, trying to stomp on Flynn's hands with his hooves.

"Ha-ha!" Flynn yelled at last. Maximus glared at Flynn.

Crack! Now they both froze as they heard the deep sound of the tree roots pulling away from the ledge. Flynn and Maximus fell, screaming and neighing, as the tree broke from the cliff.

Maximus landed hard. He was all right – but Flynn was nowhere to be found. The horse

sniffed around, trying to pick up Flynn's trail.

Carefully and quietly, Flynn moved along a steep rocky wall. He had the satchel. Now, he just had to get rid of that crazy horse! Seeing some bushes, he plunged his hand into them and parted their branches. He peered into the darkness and saw a cave. Perfect! He slipped into the entrance just as Maximus trotted by, sniffing like a bloodhound.

Turning, he saw that the cave had an opening on the opposite side; he was in a tunnel. When he emerged, he stopped short. Before him lay a beautiful valley. In the middle of the valley, a tall tower reached towards the sky. Stunned by the valley's beauty and awed by this hidden world, Flynn simply stared for a moment. He had discovered something truly marvellous.

Flynn could faintly hear Maximus at the far end of the tunnel so he raced to the tower. He pulled out some arrows and used them to hoist himself up. Moments later, Flynn climbed through the window at the top of the tower.

He had finally found a safe harbour where no royal guard or royal horse or Stabbington brother would ever find him.

BANG! Flynn's world went black.

Rapunzel stood over Flynn's unconscious body. He was the first real person she had ever seen, besides Mother Gothel. He must be a ruffian, she thought. She began looking at him.

She poked at him with the pan and then used it to turn him over. This ruffian actually looked rather nice.

She turned to Pascal. Now what should she do with the ruffian? Pascal just shrugged.

Rapunzel started to shiver all over. She had just overpowered an evil man – someone who must have come in search of her golden hair.

The man groaned and Rapunzel leaped back. She had to do something with him before he awoke, maybe lock him up in a place from which he could never escape! She took his arms and dragged him across the room. Bending and twisting his body, she pushed him in her wardrobe, then slammed the doors. She wedged a chair in front of the doors to keep them closed.

"Okay, okay," she said to herself, "I've got a person in my wardrobe." Wait. That meant – "I've got a person in my wardrobe!" She had conquered an evil, terrible monster and locked him away! This was proof that she could handle anything. She could go to see the lanterns!

Rapunzel noticed a satchel on the floor. A jewelled crown was sticking out. Rapunzel went to the mirror to see what the thing looked like on her head.

But… there was something odd about the thing. It fit snugly and felt like something that belonged on her head. Her eyes sparkled. Who was that person looking at her from the mirror?

Suddenly, a voice came from outside the

tower. "Rapunzel! Let down your hair!"

"Uh, one moment, Mother!" Rapunzel called back. Quickly she tossed the crown and the satchel into a pot.

"I have a surprise!" Mother Gothel shouted cheerfully.

"I do, too!" Rapunzel answered as she let down her hair.

"I brought back parsnips!" Mother Gothel announced. "And I'm going to make hazelnut soup for dinner. Your favourite! Surprise!"

"Well, Mother, there's something I want to tell you," Rapunzel said cautiously. "I've been thinking a lot about what you said earlier, and—"

"I hope you're not still talking about the stars," Mother Gothel said impatiently.

"Floating lights," Rapunzel said quickly, "and yes… I'm leading up to that, but—"

"Because I really thought we dropped the

issue, sweetheart."

"No, Mother," Rapunzel said. "I'm just saying, you think I'm not strong enough to handle myself out there, but—"

Mother Gothel laughed. "Oh, darling, I know you're not strong enough to handle yourself out there."

"Rapunzel, we're done talking about this," Mother Gothel snapped.

"Trust me," Rapunzel said, determined to go on with what she had to say.

"Rapunzel—" Mother Gothel was warning her.

"I know what I'm—"

"Rapunzel!" Mother Gothel shouted. *"ENOUGH WITH THE LIGHTS, RAPUNZEL! YOU ARE NOT LEAVING THIS TOWER! EVER!"*

All at once Rapunzel realized that Mother Gothel would never let her go outside. Rapunzel would be trapped at the top of the tower for the rest of her life.

Rapunzel turned and looked longingly at her mural of lights, then at her closet. Inside that closet was proof that she could handle herself in the outside world.

Inside that closet was the guide who would take her to see the sparkling lights. Mother Gothel would never have to know about it.

"All I was going to say, Mother, is that I know what I want for my birthday now."

"And what is that?" Mother Gothel asked.

"New paint," Rapunzel answered. "The paint made from the white shells you once brought me."

"Well, that's a very long trip, Rapunzel." Mother Gothel said, shaking her head, trying to dissuade Rapunzel.

"I just thought it was a better idea than the stars."

Mother Gothel's face brightened a bit. This was what she wanted to hear. "You'll be all right on your own?"

"I know I'm safe as long as I'm here," Rapunzel answered.

Mother Gothel sighed. "All right, then. I'll be back in three days' time," she said.

Rapunzel watched from her window until Mother Gothel disappeared into the forest. Then, using her hair, she pulled the wardrobe doors open.

The man in the closet was still unconscious. Quickly, Rapunzel sat him on a chair. Then she firmly tied him up with her hair.

Pascal jumped on the man and tried waking him by slapping his face with his little tail. No response. Pascal looked at Rapunzel. She urged him on. Pascal slapped his tail against the man's cheek again. Still no response.

Pascal thought for a moment. Then he

slipped his long tongue into the man's ear.

"Blll-AHH!" Flynn awoke abruptly. Pascal's tongue was gross and – and it tickled!

"Struggling is pointless, I know what you're here for," Rapunzel said firmly, brandishing her pan, "and I'm not afraid of you."

"What?" Flynn answered, confused by it all.

"Who are you and how did you find me?" Rapunzel asked him.

Flynn hesitated and Rapunzel raised her pan. "Okay, okay, all right," he said quickly, not wanting to be hit on the head again.

Flynn tried to be charming. "I know not who you are, nor how I came to find you, but may I just say…? Hi." Flynn raised an eyebrow and gave Rapunzel a devilish grin. "The name's Flynn Rider. How's your day going?"

Rapunzel had no idea what the man was trying to do, but he looked really weird.

"Who else knows my location, Flynn Rider?"

Flynn sighed. "I was…" Flynn stopped short, filled with alarm. "…Where is my satchel?"

"I've hidden it somewhere you'll never find it," Rapunzel said confidently.

Flynn quickly surveyed the room and glanced at Rapunzel, and said: "It's in that pot, isn't it?"

BANG! She hit him again. Quickly, she looked around to hide the satchel again. She lifted a loose board in the stairs and stashed the satchel underneath.

A few minutes later, Pascal flicked his tongue

into Flynn's ear again and he awoke with a jump. "Would you stop that!" Flynn yelled, squirming.

Rapunzel just smiled and said, "Now it's hidden where you'll never find it."

She paced around him, wrapping him ever more tightly in her long hair.

"So, what do you want with my hair? To cut it?" she asked accusingly. "To sell it?"

"No! Listen, the only thing I want to do with your hair is get out of it," Flynn said. "Literally."

"Wait. You don't want my hair?" Rapunzel asked in disbelief.

"Why on earth would I want your hair?" Flynn asked. "Look, I was being chased, I saw a tower, and I climbed it. End of story."

Rapunzel eyed him. If he didn't want her hair, then she could trust him!

"Okay, Flynn Rider," she said finally. "I'm prepared to offer you a deal."

"Deal?" Flynn said, willing to listen.

"Do you know what these are?" she asked, stepping up on the mantel above the fireplace. She pulled back the curtain, revealing the mural of the floating lights.

Flynn nodded. "You mean the lantern thing they do for the princess?"

"Well, tomorrow night, they will light the night sky with these lanterns. You will act as my guide, take me to the castle and return me home safely. Then, and only then, will I return your satchel to you. That is my deal."

Flynn refused.

"You can tear this tower apart brick-by-brick, but without my help, you will never find your precious satchel."

"I take you to see the lanterns, bring you back home and you'll give me back my satchel?"

Rapunzel nodded, adding, "I promise. And when I promise something, I never, ever break that promise. Ever."

Flynn knew he could not go to the kingdom –
not now! He was a wanted thief. So he changed
his strategy. Confidently, he pursed his lips and
oh-so-carefully raised one eyebrow. He knew
this was his most handsome expression.

Nothing happened.

Rapunzel waited for something to happen.
She had no idea what Flynn was doing.

"This is kind of an off day for me," Flynn said,
beginning to doubt himself.

"Fine," he said finally, "I'll take you to see
the lanterns."

"Really?" Rapunzel exclaimed. This. Was. It!
She was going to see the lights!

A little while later, Flynn, unbound and freed
from Rapunzel's hair, began to climb down the
tower the same way he had come up, using
his arrows.

Halfway down, he looked up. Rapunzel was

standing in the window. She was still holding her pan in case of any trouble. She hadn't moved an inch.

"You coming?" Flynn shouted up at her.

Rapunzel arranged her hair to let herself down from the tower safely. Pascal gave her a thumbs-up for courage.

Turning, she looked back at her mural and it gave her confidence.

Slowly, she rapelled down the tower for the first time. At the bottom of the tower, her toes touched the soft grass. She was standing on the ground for the first time in her life! It felt wonderful. The sky looked enormous. The sunlight shimmered through the trees. It smelled fresh. Outside was great!

"Woo-hoo!" Rapunzel shouted, dancing in the sunlight. "I can't believe I did this! I can't believe I did this!"

Chapter 3

"This is incredible!" Rapunzel said as she and Flynn walked deeper into the forest. Then she remembered how her mother would feel if she knew she'd disobeyed her.

"Mother would be so furious." She looked at Flynn and said, "But it's okay. I mean, what she doesn't know won't kill her, right?" Flynn just shrugged and nodded.

Rapunzel knelt down to look at some leaves and mud on the forest floor. Everything was new and beautiful to her. "This is so fun!" she said.

Then she saw a hill. A big, grassy hill. It looked… fun! She threw herself on her back and rolled down the hill, filled with delight.

"Best! Day! Ever!"

Finally, remembering Mother Gothel again, she slumped against a boulder and sobbed.

Flynn sat down next to her.

"You know," he said gently, "I can't help but notice… you seem a little at war with yourself here."

"What?" Rapunzel asked feebly.

Flynn moved closer, trying to seem gentle. He had an idea.

"I'm just picking up bits and pieces," he said to her softly, in a sugary-sweet voice. "Overprotective mother. Forbidden road trip.

I mean, this is serious stuff. But let me ease your conscience: this is part of growing up. A little rebellion, a little adventure, that's good! Healthy, even!"

"You think?" Rapunzel perked up a little.

"I know!" Flynn said confidently. "You're way overthinking this. Trust me. Does your mother deserve it? No. Would this break her heart and crush her soul? Of course. But you've just got to do it!"

"She would be heartbroken," Rapunzel concluded.

Flynn tried to look as distressed as Rapunzel. He had her wrapped around his little finger!

"Oh, bother. All right, I can't believe I'm saying this, but – I'm letting you out of the deal."

"What?" Rapunzel said. She knew she probably should go back to Mother Gothel, but she liked it outside. Nobody had hurt her.

Flynn started to lead her back towards the tower.

"Don't thank me," he was saying. "Let's just

get you home. I get back my satchel, you get back a mother-daughter relationship based on mutual trust and voilà! We part ways as unlikely friends."

Rapunzel pulled herself together. "No. No," she said firmly. "I'm seeing those lanterns."

"Oh, c'mon!" Flynn whined. "What is it going to take for me to get my satchel back?"

Just then, something rustled through the bushes. Rapunzel jumped, terrified.

"Is it ruffians? Have they come for me?" She leaped behind Flynn for protection.

A fuzzy rabbit jumped out of the bushes. Rapunzel blushed.

"Probably be best if we avoid ruffians and thugs?" Flynn asked.

Rapunzel agreed, "That'd probably be best."

Flynn suddenly had an idea. "Are you hungry?" he said with a devious smile, "I know a great place for lunch."

"Where?" Rapunzel asked.

"Oh, don't worry," Flynn told her, grinning. "You'll know it when you smell it."

In another part of the forest, Maximus, the palace guard horse, was still eagerly sniffing the ground for Flynn Rider. Maximus was not used to failing in a chase and he definitely was not going to fail in this one.

Maximus sniffed the air, trying to pick up the scoundrel's scent. Suddenly, his ears perked up. There was a rustling in the bushes. *Aha!* The horse hid behind a large green bush, ready to catch that man. A figure, dark and shadowy, approached. When the figure got just close enough, he leaped out to confront it. It wasn't Flynn he found – he was face to face with Mother Gothel!

Maximus looked confused.

Mother Gothel was wondering the same thing about the horse. Startled at first, she quickly noticed the kingdom's emblem on the horse's bridle.

"A palace horse?" she mumbled to herself. "Where is your rider?" The palace guards rarely came around this area of the forest, not since—

"Oh, no," Mother Gothel gasped. "Rapunzel!" In a panic, Mother Gothel turned and ran back toward the tower. When she got there, she called out, "Rapunzel? Rapunzel! Let down your hair!"

But no one answered.

She ran to the back of the tower. Long ago, she had used this entrance. Now, she ripped at the branches that had grown over the door and uncovered the hidden entrance.

Climbing a secret staircase, Mother Gothel burst through a door hidden in the floor. The tower was empty.

"Rapunzel!" she called out desperately. Then

she saw a glint of something under the stairs. She moved towards it, ripped the board away and found a satchel hidden underneath. Much to her horror, she found the crown of the lost princess inside. Then she saw the WANTED poster with Flynn Rider's picture on it.

Mother Gothel wasted no time. She grabbed a dagger and the satchel and quickly left the empty tower.

Chapter 4

*M*eanwhile, Flynn and Rapunzel were still searching for a place to eat.

"Ah, there it is!" Flynn exclaimed at last. "The Snuggly Duckling!"

Rapunzel stared at the little tavern. It looked interesting.

"Don't worry," Flynn said. "It's a very quaint place, perfect for you. Don't want you getting scared and giving up on this whole endeavour, now, do we?"

He was determined to terrify that girl right back to her tower, retrieve his crown and cash it in.

"Well, I do like ducklings," Rapunzel said.

"Who doesn't?" Flynn said brightly. "Garçon!" He shouted to the greasy tavern keeper as they entered the ramshackle establishment. "Your finest table, please!"

The tavern was dark and musty inside. It was noisy too, filled with the sounds of men yelling and fighting, laughing and grumbling. Rapunzel's eyes widened. A silence fell over the room as she and Flynn entered. When her eyes adjusted to the gloom, she looked around. The tavern was filled with a large group of terrifying, brutish men!

Ruffians and thugs! Rapunzel's heart raced. *They want my hair!* Suddenly, she felt someone grab a piece of her hair.

"That's a lot of hair," the thug said menacingly.

"Is that blood in your moustache?" Flynn asked another, smaller thug. "Look at this, look at all the blood in his moustache!"

Rapunzel backed away in terror and bumped

into another thug. "Sorry," she said to the man. "Sorry."

Flynn could see that Rapunzel was as white as a ghost. His plan was working. "Hey, you don't look so good, Blondie. Maybe we should get you home, call it a day?" he suggested hopefully.

"Okay." Rapunzel nodded.

"Probably better off doing just that." Flynn shrugged. "This is a five-star joint, after all. And if you can't handle this place, well, maybe you should be back in your tower."

Flynn had opened the door to leave when a

huge hand grabbed the door and slammed it. The hand slapped the WANTED poster of Flynn onto the door.

"Is this you?" the huge man said.

Now Flynn turned pale.

Every thug in the room eyed the reward mentioned on the poster. All heads turned in Flynn's direction with a keen interest.

"It's him, all right," one thug said. "Greno, go find some guards."

"That reward's gonna buy me a new hook," a one-armed thug said, licking his chops.

A brawl quickly ensued, with bottles crashing and chairs flying. Everyone was pulling at Flynn. Pascal and Rapunzel ducked and cringed, terrified.

"Please!" Flynn squealed from under the pile of filthy men. "We can work this out!"

Rapunzel tried to help. She raised her frying pan and spoke up. "Um, excuse me? Ruffians?

Gentlemen! Please! Is it possible to just get my guide back?" Rapunzel shouted. She poked one of the thugs with her pan. "Just stop. Stop!" Nothing happened.

It was time to take action! She whacked her pan against a giant pot hanging from the ceiling. CLANG! Then, with all her might, she yelled, "PUT HIM DOWN!"

For a moment, there was absolute silence. Rapunzel took a breath. "Okay," she said to the rabid mob, "I don't know where I am and I need him to take me to see the lanterns because I've been dreaming about them my entire life! Find your humanity!" she pleaded. "Haven't you ever had a dream?"

Flynn cringed. Did she really want to talk about dreams with this crowd? He was definitely going to end up with a broken nose.

Then the thug with a hook for a hand moved towards Rapunzel with a menacing look.

Rapunzel froze.

"I had a dream once," the brute said softly. He tossed aside his axe and told Rapunzel that he'd dreamed of being a pianist.

Flynn was becoming more and more interested. What was up with this young woman, anyway? He watched as the tavern thugs turned to mush, weeping and sweetly telling Rapunzel about their dreams. Everyone seemed to adore her!

Unfortunately, something terribly serious was happening outside.

Mother Gothel had tracked Rapunzel and

Flynn to the Snuggly Duckling. When she looked through the window, she was stunned. Rapunzel was happily mingling with those thugs! Mother Gothel felt her world crumbling around her.

Inside, the crowd finally turned to Flynn Rider. "What about you?" the man with the hook for a hand asked. "What's your dream?"

Flynn told them about his dream of living on his own island. The thugs roared their approval and tossed Flynn in the air.

Outside, spying through the window, Mother Gothel controlled herself. She had to focus her energies on formulating a plan to get Rapunzel back to the tower.

Hearing a noise behind her, she swiftly ducked into the shadows. A group of angry palace guards raced past her and burst into the Snuggly Duckling.

"Where's Rider?" the captain of the guards

barked. "Where is he? I know he's in here somewhere." The captain surveyed the mangy crowd in the tavern.

Flynn grabbed Rapunzel, with Pascal still clinging to her hair, and ducked behind the counter. Peeking over the top, Flynn saw the palace guards bring in the Stabbington brothers. Their hands were in shackles. Then he saw Maximus clomp into the tavern and begin sniffing around.

Someone reached down and grabbed Flynn and Rapunzel. Flynn cringed, thinking he was done for. But the thug lifted a hidden door in the floor, revealing a secret passageway.

"Go live your dream," the thug said sweetly.

"I will," Flynn told him, finding this turn of events bizarre but good. Really good!

"Your dream stinks," the thug bluntly told Flynn. "I was talking to her." Rapunzel smiled at the thug as Flynn entered the secret passageway.

"Are you coming, Blondie?" Flynn asked her.

Rapunzel looked into the dank tunnel and followed Flynn.

Inside the tavern, the royal guards continued their search.

Maximus had picked up that scoundrel's scent and he followed it until he saw a slight irregularity in the floorboards. He knocked his hoof against the floor and a door swung open.

Aha!

"A passage?" the captain said, coming up behind Maximus. "Come on, men. Let's go!" Before the captain entered the tunnel, he turned

towards the Stabbington brothers.

"Conli, make sure those boys don't get away," the captain said to one of his guards. The guard nodded and the captain disappeared into the tunnel.

BAM! The brothers head-butted the guard hard and they headed toward the tunnel.

Outside the tavern, Mother Gothel was still watching. When she finally saw a thug stumble out the door of the Snuggly Duckling alone, Mother Gothel stepped from the shadows.

"Excuse me, sir," she said, using her most caring voice. "I am desperately trying to find my daughter. Where does that tunnel let out?"

Chapter 5

*I*nside the tunnel and happy to be making his escape, Flynn led the way.

"You know," he said to Rapunzel awkwardly, embarrassed to have been rescued by a girl, "for the record, I had everything very under control."

But even as he spoke, the cavern began to shake. Debris sifted down on their heads.

Rapunzel turned and saw Maximus charging

down the tunnel towards them. The guardsmen were right behind him.

"Flynn!" she cried out.

One of the guards spotted them and shouted, "Rider!"

Flynn chose to respond to Rapunzel: "Run!"

Flynn and Rapunzel dashed down the tunnel to the end of the passageway. The palace guards and the Stabbingtons were still chasing them. Just as it looked as if Rapunzel and Flynn were about to escape, a furious Maximus kicked a large board from a dam to create a bridge so he could cross the cavern to Flynn. It also meant that water began leaking from the dam, threatening an explosive flood at any moment.

The crash of the dam bursting was earth-shaking. Water roared into the cavern.

The powerful moving wall of water knocked down a pillar as Flynn ran. Dashing at top speed, he caught up with Rapunzel and Pascal. Flynn grabbed an armload of Rapunzel's hair as the two ran for cover. The pillar crashed down just behind them as they ducked into the cave.

Flynn and Rapunzel were safe for now, but the cave's entrance was blocked by the rubble from the fallen pillar. Flynn, Rapunzel and little Pascal were now sealed inside a rocky cavern.

The sealed cavern did not protect them from the rushing water. Within minutes, Flynn and Rapunzel were waist deep in water that was rising quickly. Flynn dove down, searching for an exit. He hardly noticed the huge gash on his hand as he grasped for any opening among the jagged rocks.

"It's no use," he said, gasping, as he emerged from the dark water. "I can't see anything. It's pitch black down there."

Flynn and Rapunzel looked at each other helplessly. Having come so far together, they

would die together in this little cave.

"This is all my fault," Rapunzel said. "Mother Gothel was right. I never should have done this. I'm so sorry, Flynn."

"Eugene," he said as he grasped Rapunzel's hand. "My real name's Eugene Fitzherbert. Someone might as well know."

After a moment of silence, Rapunzel blurted out her own secret: "I have magic hair that glows when I sing."

Flynn stared at her speechlessly as she began to sing. Within moments, her hair started to glow, lighting up the cave.

Rapunzel took a deep breath and dove underwater, lighting their way. Following her, Flynn saw a small opening in the corner of the cave. Yanking at stones with all his energy, Flynn broke through at last.

The water burst through the opening, carrying Flynn and Rapunzel out into the river.

Coughing and gasping for air, Rapunzel, Pascal and Flynn threw themselves onto the riverbank.

"I'm alive!" Rapunzel choked out.

Flynn looked at Pascal. Flynn was pale and his eyes were wide with disbelief. "Her hair glows!" Flynn stifled a tiny shriek as he spoke to Pascal.

"I'm alive!" Rapunzel screamed joyfully.

"Why does her hair glow?" Flynn asked Pascal, but the chameleon could only shrug.

"Eugene!" Rapunzel shouted, trying to get his attention.

"What?" Flynn shouted in reply. He was still in shock, trying to figure it all out. Rapunzel stared at Flynn's injured hand. It looked terrible.

Rapunzel sighed. Flynn was freaked out by her, but she needed to help him.

"It doesn't just glow," she added.

Having found her exit of the tunnel overground, Mother Gothel waited with her long dagger hidden in her cloak. When the tunnel door finally opened, it wasn't Flynn Rider and Rapunzel who came out – it was the Stabbington brothers. Mother Gothel quickly ducked behind a tree.

"I'll kill him. I'll kill that Rider," the talking Stabbington said angrily to his brother. "We'll cut him off at the kingdom and get back the crown. Come on!"

"Or perhaps you want to stop acting like wild dogs chasing their tails and think for a moment?" Mother Gothel rasped from her hiding place.

The startled Stabbington brothers drew their swords.

"There's no need for that." She tossed them the satchel she had found in the tower and

watched as they removed the crown and smiled broadly. She hoped they could help her, so she tempted them with something better....

At that same moment, Rapunzel took Flynn's injured hand and began wrapping her hair around it.

"Flynn. Please," Rapunzel said soothingly. "Just... don't... freak out."

Slowly, she began to sing and her hair began to glow. Flynn gazed in amazement but stayed

silent. Something was happening to his injured hand. He could feel it….

When she finished, she gently pulled her hair from Flynn's palm. He looked at Pascal. The little chameleon signalled to him to look at his hand. It was completely healed!

Then, controlling himself, he said: "So, that's pretty neat – what your hair does. How long has that been going on, exactly?"

"I don't know." Rapunzel sighed. But she did trust Flynn. "People tried to cut it once when I was younger. They wanted to take it themselves. But when it's cut, it loses its power. A gift like that? It has to be protected. That's why I never left the…"

Finally understanding, Flynn finished her sentence. "You never left that tower." The revelation both shocked him and made him want to protect her. "And you're still going to go back?"

"No!" Rapunzel replied. Then she said, "Yes. Ughhhhh!" She buried her face in her hands. "It's complicated."

Quickly, she changed the subject. She wanted to know more about who the Flynn Rider was that Eugene had named himself after. It turned out that Flynn was the richest, most powerful man in the world. He could do anything and go anywhere he wanted. He was a man in a book that Flynn – or rather, Eugene – had read about every night when he was a child. Over time, Eugene had adopted the name as his own.

When he finished with his story, Flynn stood

up and stretched. "I need to get some more firewood," he said. Promising to return soon, he wandered off into the pitch-black forest.

Rapunzel heard a darkly familiar voice behind her. Startled, she turned to face the cloaked and hooded visitor.

"Hello, dear," Mother Gothel said.

"What… what are you doing here?" Rapunzel said, fumbling for words. "I mean, how did you find me?"

Mother Gothel walked up to Rapunzel and gave her hug. "Oh, it was easy, really," she said. "I just listened for the sound of complete and

utter betrayal and followed that."

"We're going home, Rapunzel," Mother Gothel commanded. "Now."

"You don't understand," Rapunzel said. "I've been on this incredible journey, and I've seen and learned so much! I even met someone."

"Yes. The wanted thief." Mother Gothel frowned with disgust.

"No, Mother, wait! I think he likes me."

"Likes you!" Mother Gothel scoffed. "This whole romance that you've invented just proves that you're too naïve to be here. Why would he like you, really?"

Rapunzel had heard Mother Gothel's scornful dismissals before. She had even accepted them. But she no longer believed them – Mother Gothel had lied to her throughout her life.

"Come, come," Mother Gothel said. "You know that I'm right." She tossed the crown to Rapunzel.

Rapunzel began to wonder: If she gave the

crown to Flynn, would he leave her alone and run away with his prized crown?

"No," Rapunzel said firmly.

The firelight flashed across Mother Gothel's face as it filled with rage.

"Don't say I didn't warn you. Show him this. Then see how much he likes you!"

"I will!" Rapunzel said defiantly.

Mother Gothel simply turned her back and disappeared into the dark forest.

Meanwhile, the Stabbington brothers were hiding in the woods with Mother Gothel. They wanted to grab Flynn, the crown and the girl with the golden hair right then and there, but Mother Gothel held them back.

"Patience, boys," she whispered. "Trust me, it's all going exactly to plan."

Chapter 6

As the sun rose over their little campsite, Flynn Rider was fast asleep. He didn't notice that Maximus had finally found him. Again. Maximus nipped at Flynn's sleeve as Flynn jumped to his feet.

Rapunzel awoke to a scream. The tenacious horse now had hold of Flynn's foot and was dragging him away!

Astonished at the sight, Rapunzel tried to help, grabbing Flynn's arms. Soon Rapunzel and Maximus were engaged in a tug-of-war with Flynn stretched between them.

"Don't worry, Blondie!" Flynn said, trying to sound as if he were in control. "I've got him right where I want him!"

"Give me him!" She and the horse were pulling Flynn in opposite directions when Flynn wiggled his foot out of the boot in Maximus's mouth. Flynn scrambled away. Maximus charged after him.

Rapunzel stepped in front of the horse.

"Whoa, boy, easy. That's it," Rapunzel said sweetly. "Now sit." Maximus hesitated. But Rapunzel looked him in the eye and said again, "Sit."

This time Maximus sat. Rapunzel smiled. "You're such a good boy," she said, patting the horse's neck. "Yes, you are. Now drop the boot."

The boot instantly fell from the horse's mouth. Rapunzel patted him gently. "Oh, look at you, all wet and tired. Are you tired from chasing this bad man all over the place?"

Flynn rolled his eyes. "You've got to be kidding me." Then he cringed just a bit. Am I actually jealous of a horse? *Ugh!*

Rapunzel looked into the horse's big eyes and explained everything very sweetly to him.

"Today is the biggest day of my life," she said. Maximus nodded. "And the thing is, I want you not to get Flynn arrested. Just for twenty-four hours and then you can chase each other to your hearts' content. Okay?" Rapunzel paused. "And it's also my birthday – just so you know."

Carefully, Rapunzel guided Maximus and Flynn together. She wanted them to shake hoof and hand in a truce.

The horse snorted and finally raised his hoof. Flynn grudgingly reached out to shake it.

It was the beginning of a perfect day, Rapunzel thought. She couldn't wait. Today she would visit the kingdom – and later see those lights at last.

Before long, Rapunzel and Flynn reached the kingdom's gates. Pascal rode atop Maximus's head, grasping his ears and using them as reins.

As they approached a bridge and a group of palace guards, Flynn worried that he might be recognized and arrested, but Maximus was determined to take care of everything.

Hoping Rapunzel would notice his cleverness, Maximus spied a boy up ahead holding an armful of small kingdom flags. Maximus went into action, hoisting the boy into Flynn's arms. With a mass of flags shielding Flynn's face, they easily walked past the guards. Maximus glanced proudly at Rapunzel.

"Good morning!" Rapunzel cheerfully

greeted the guards.

And then, all at once, Rapunzel was inside the village. She could hardly contain her excitement. It was a wonderful afternoon and before they knew it, the town crier called out from a stage at the centre of the village:

"It is time, good people! Gather around! Yes, come, gather around! Today we dance to celebrate our lost princess."

As the man spoke, a mosaic depicting the King and Queen caught Rapunzel's eye. She couldn't help gazing at the picture of the royal couple

holding their baby – a portrait from the time just before the princess was stolen from them. For some reason, Rapunzel felt mesmerized by the emerald-green eyes of the Queen and the little lost princess wearing the crown. The Queen looked almost exactly like Rapunzel.

Flynn twirled Rapunzel in time to the music. They separated and danced with other partners. Then they came together again – and their eyes locked. Just when Rapunzel thought it couldn't be more magical, the town crier shouted, "To the boats!"

The entire, wonderful day had passed and now night was falling. It was time to release the lanterns.

Rapunzel gave Maximus a wave as Flynn guided her aboard a boat and rowed away from the docks.

"Where are we going?" Rapunzel asked him.

"Well, if it's the best day of your life," Flynn replied, "you might as well have the best seat in the house."

Rapunzel turned back towards the docks and saw the kingdom laid out before her.

"Oh, this is perfect!" she exclaimed.

"So, are you excited?"

"I'm thinking that I'm terrified," Rapunzel replied. "What if it's not everything I dreamed it would be?"

Flynn smiled. "It will be."

"And what if it is?" Rapunzel asked, feeling overwhelmed by it all. "What do I do then?"

"That's the good part, I guess," Flynn said as

they gazed at the kingdom together. "You get to go find a new dream."

From their balcony inside the palace courtyard, the King and Queen launched the first lantern. Thousands of lanterns followed the first, filling the sky! It was as if she and Flynn were floating in a sea of stars.

Then Rapunzel turned to Flynn and saw that he had a lantern in his hands. He had bought it in the village and hidden it in the boat, waiting for this moment to surprise Rapunzel with the gift.

Rapunzel was so thrilled, she rushed to him and held the lantern.

"I can't believe I'm really here!" she exclaimed. "I don't know what it is, but I feel like I belong here."

Reaching down, she grabbed Flynn's satchel. "I have something for you too," she said, handing it to him. "I should have given it to you before. But I was just scared. And the thing is, I'm not scared anymore. You know what I mean?" She wanted Flynn to understand.

"Yeah. Yeah, I do," Flynn said truthfully. He knew that the crown was still in that satchel, but it no longer meant that much to him. Quickly, he turned back to Rapunzel. Holding the lantern together, they released it into the sky.

Then Flynn leaned in closer.

He stopped just short of kissing Rapunzel. He glanced over her shoulder. The Stabbington brothers were on the shore, waiting for him.

"Is everything, okay?" Rapunzel asked.

"Yes… yes, of course," Flynn said, not wanting to ruin the day for her. He started rowing back towards the shore to face the Stabbington brothers.

"I'm sorry," he said. "Everything's fine, but there's just something I have to take care of."

Rapunzel, their journey together, all of it had changed Flynn's view of the world. He wanted to make things right. He was in love with Rapunzel. He no longer wanted to be a thief, a lone highwayman always running away from everything.

Flynn landed the boat on the shore and leaped out. He told Rapunzel to wait for him.

Flynn tossed the satchel down in front of the Stabbingtons.

"There," he said as the crown fell out of the bag and onto the ground. "You got what you wanted. Now leave us alone. I never want to see

you again." Flynn turned to leave.

"Holding out on us again, eh, Rider?" said the one Stabbington as his brother sneaked up behind Flynn.

"What?" Flynn was confused, but one thing was for sure: the Stabbington brothers were not just interested in the crown anymore.

Chapter 7

*I*n a menacing tone, the Stabbington without the eye patch told Flynn everything that he and his brother had learned from wicked Mother Gothel.

"We heard you found something. Something much more valuable than a crown."

A little while later, Rapunzel was relieved to see a man finally step from the bushes.

"I was starting to think you ran off with the crown and left me!" she said with a laugh, thinking it was Flynn.

"He did," a rough voice answered. Rapunzel gasped. She wasn't looking at Flynn. And she wasn't looking at just one man, but two – the Stabbington brothers.

"What?" Rapunzel said, confused and panicked. "No, he wouldn't."

"See for yourself!" the talking brother replied, pointing toward the water.

Rapunzel looked and saw Flynn standing at the helm of a small ship.

She called to him, but Flynn didn't call back or turn to look at her. Rapunzel was crushed.

The brutish men behind her laughed. "A fair trade: a crown for the girl with the magic hair," the one brother said. "How much do you think someone would pay to stay young and healthy forever?"

"No. No, please. No!" Rapunzel shouted as the brothers approached. She ran as fast as she could into the darkness.

From behind her, she heard a loud clatter and some thumps.

"Oh, my precious girl!" Mother Gothel said, brimming with emotion. The Stabbington brothers lay at her feet, knocked unconscious.

"Mother?" Rapunzel gasped. Mother Gothel threw her arms around the girl. Rapunzel hugged Mother Gothel too and finally broke down and cried.

"You were right, Mother," she said, nodding. Her eyes were blank and her heart was numb. "I'll never leave you again." Rapunzel had never felt such deep sorrow in her entire life.

Out in the harbour, the ship was now moving towards the dock, but not because Flynn was steering it. The Stabbingtons had knocked him unconscious and tied him to the mast.

Following Mother Gothel's instructions, the

brothers had tied the crown tightly to Flynn's hand. They knew what would happen when the palace guards found the drifting ship. Flynn Rider would be going off to jail.

Flynn was still unconscious when the current slammed the small ship into the dock.

Flynn was jolted awake just in time to see the palace guards running towards him. He looked around in confusion, having no idea how he was on the ship.

Then he heard a palace guard say, "Look! The crown!"

Flynn remembered the Stabbington brothers. Flynn knew they must have set him up, but all he cared about was what had happened to Rapunzel.

"Rapunzel? Rapunzel!" Flynn shouted out desperately.

The only witness to the whole sequence of events was Maximus. He snorted angrily and followed as the guards hauled Flynn off to the palace jail. Then he galloped straight towards the gates of the kingdom – he had to find help.

While the guards were busy locking up Flynn, Mother Gothel led Rapunzel back to the tower.

Rapunzel went directly to her loft. Pascal still clung to her hair near her shoulder, hoping to help somehow, but Rapunzel was dazed by everything that had happened. She couldn't believe Flynn had taken the crown and left her.

As she slumped at the edge of her bed, her hand strayed to her pocket, from which she pulled out a small kingdom flag – purple, with a gold sun on it. She stared at the flag and sighed, thinking of Flynn, the friendly thugs in the tavern, the people in the kingdom.

Rapunzel looked at her painted wall. That sun seemed to be everywhere, showing up in bright spots on the painting. The kingdom's sun fit into every small blank place on her mural. All these years, without realizing it, Rapunzel had been incorporating the outline of the golden

sun in the empty spaces of the picture!

A flood of images suddenly filled Rapunzel's head. She recalled Flynn saying that the lights were floating lanterns that the kingdom sent up every year on the lost princess's birthday – her birthday. She remembered the mosaic of the royal family. The King and Queen were holding the lost princess. The Queen and the baby both had green eyes just like Rapunzel's. She remembered her reflection in the mirror when she placed the crown on her head.

Rapunzel, at last, knew exactly who she was.

"Rapunzel, what's going on up there? Are you all right?" Mother Gothel asked impatiently.

Mother Gothel's eyes grew wide when she saw Rapunzel standing above her on the stairs.

"I'm the lost princess," Rapunzel said softly.

Mother Gothel tried to dismiss it all. "Oh, please speak up, Rapunzel. You know I hate mumbling," she snapped.

"I am the lost princess, aren't I?" Rapunzel repeated loudly and clearly. "Did I mumble, Mother?"

Rapunzel walked past Mother Gothel and went down the stairs. Mother Gothel had been lying to her ever since she had stolen her away from her true parents.

"It was you!" Rapunzel said coldly. Now she was thinking of Flynn. Mother Gothel had set him up. "It was all you!"

"Everything I did was to protect you," Mother Gothel said, pleading with Rapunzel. "Where will you go?" she suddenly asked sharply. "He won't be there for you!"

Rapunzel turned and looked at her. "What did you do to him?" she demanded. She felt her heart swell, her love for Flynn giving her the courage to stand up to Mother Gothel at last.

"That criminal is to be hanged for his crimes," Mother Gothel said cruelly.

"No," Rapunzel murmured, horrified. "No."

Mother Gothel could see that Rapunzel was upset and she moved closer to make the most of the opportunity.

"Now, now. It's all right," Mother Gothel said in her most soothing voice. She held out her arms as she always had. "All is as it should be."

"How could you do this? I love him," Rapunzel said.

"I know you think you do, dear," she said in her silkiest, most soothing voice.

"No," Rapunzel said firmly as she grasped Mother Gothel's outstretched arm. "You were wrong about the world, Mother. And you were wrong about me. I am not stupid, and I am not small. And I will never let you use my hair again!" Rapunzel twisted Mother Gothel's arm and pushed her away. The older woman stumbled backward and crashed into her full-length mirror. The mirror shattered.

She had given Rapunzel her chance to go back to the way things used to be. Now Mother Gothel would use stronger means to keep the girl with the golden hair imprisoned.

In the kingdom's jail, Flynn sat in his cell, wondering where Rapunzel was and whether she was hurt or in trouble. He blamed himself. If he hadn't stolen the crown, he never would have gotten mixed up with those Stabbington brothers.

"Let's get this over with, Rider," a jail guard announced as he unlocked the cell door. Flynn knew he was in trouble. After all, he had stolen the lost princess's crown. The punishment was death by hanging.

Still, he was more worried about Rapunzel. As two guards escorted him through the jail, Flynn spotted the Stabbingtons in one of the cells.

"How did you know about her? Tell me, NOW!"

"It wasn't us. It was the old lady."

Flynn tightened his grip, but the guards rushed up and pulled him back roughly.

Suddenly he heard a ruckus outside. Flynn's jaw dropped. The thugs from the Snuggly Duckling had arrived and they had come to break Flynn out of jail! Flynn didn't know how or why they had come, but he leaped at the opportunity.

Swinging his chains, he knocked over the

two guards. He and the thugs raced outside
and headed toward the kingdom's gates. One
of the thugs grabbed Flynn and put him on
a wheelbarrow. Then, using the barrow as a
seesaw, another thug jumped on the other end,
launching Flynn into the air. He landed perfectly
on Maximus's back.

"Shut the gates! Shut the gates! Shut the
gates!" the guards yelled. Maximus charged!
The speedy horse zipped right through the
gates as they slammed shut. Safely outside,
Flynn and Maximus raced to save Rapunzel.

Chapter 8

"Rapunzel, let down your hair!" Flynn yelled, desperately hoping she was safe.

Swoosh! Rapunzel's long blonde hair glided out of the window and down the tower. Grasping her hair, Flynn climbed up the tower as fast as he could. At last, he made it to the window and hauled himself inside.

"Rapunzel, I thought I'd never see you again!" Flynn exclaimed.

Then he stopped short and gasped. In the darkness, he saw the shards of a broken mirror on the floor – and heard the muffled sound of Rapunzel's voice. She was kneeling on the floor across from him. Mother Gothel had chained her to the wall and gagged her. Rapunzel's eyes were wide with fear as she struggled to warn him.

Then Flynn felt the sharp point of Mother Gothel's dagger against his back. He crumpled to the floor in pain.

Rapunzel cried out through the rags stuffed in her mouth. But Mother Gothel stared at her coldly and said,

"Now look what you've done, Rapunzel. Oh, don't you worry, dear. Our secret will die with him."

Rapunzel needed to save him with her hair!

Mother Gothel unfastened Rapunzel's chains and dragged her towards the secret trapdoor in the floor.

"And as for us, we are going where no will ever find you." Mother Gothel yanked Rapunzel, who was struggling against her with all her might.

"Rapunzel! Really!" Mother Gothel shouted. "Enough already! STOP FIGHTING ME!"

But Rapunzel did fight – as hard as she could – until the rags fell from her mouth.

"No!" Rapunzel cried out in defiance. "I won't stop! For every minute, for the rest of my life, I will fight!" Rapunzel was stronger now, stronger than she ever had been. At last she knew the truth. She knew everything, and she understood everything clearly.

"I will never stop trying to get away from you." She drew a deep breath, refusing to take her eyes off Mother Gothel. And she made her choice. "If you let me save him, I will go with you."

"No!" Flynn cried out. Rapunzel needed to be free from this woman. "No, Rapunzel!"

Rapunzel kept her gaze on Mother Gothel.

"I'll never run," Rapunzel promised. "I'll never try to escape. Just let me heal him. And you and I will be together. Forever. Just like you want."

Rapunzel knew that her promise meant she would never see Flynn again, but at least she would know that he was alive, living outside in the beautiful world filled with wonderful, kind people. Her voice barely a whisper, she repeated, "Just let me heal him."

Mother Gothel's eyes narrowed for a moment before she let Rapunzel go.

"Rapunzel, no!" he said weakly. "I can't let you…." His voice faded as he clutched a shard of the broken mirror. He would rather die than have the lovely, spirited Rapunzel live the rest of her life imprisoned in some secret tower with

Mother Gothel.

Using his last ounce of strength, Flynn reached up and, in one swift motion, cut off Rapunzel's hair.

The long golden locks fell to the floor and turned brown, depleted of their magic.

"No! What have you done? NO!" Stumbling, Mother Gothel staggered across the room. She was aging rapidly, and quickly disintegrated into nothing more than a pile of dust.

But Rapunzel was looking at Flynn. He was dying, and there was no magic left in her hair to save him!

"Oh, no! Eugene! Don't go. Stay with me!" she sobbed. "Don't leave me. I can't do this without you."

"Hey," Flynn whispered with his last breaths. "You were my new dream."

"And you were mine too." Rapunzel leaned towards Flynn as he closed his eyes.

Distraught, Rapunzel could not hold back her grief. She wept, cradling Flynn's limp body.

A single golden tear fell on his cheek.

Flynn stirred. Though she didn't know it, Rapunzel did have one last bit of magic left deep inside her and it was contained in that single golden tear. Flynn's eyes fluttered open.

"Rapunzel!" he whispered.

"Eugene!"

Flynn was alive!

Rapunzel returned to the kingdom with Flynn by her side. Clutching Flynn's hand, Rapunzel followed a royal escort to the palace. Soon they entered the throne room.

And then she saw them: the King and Queen. Rapunzel looked into their eyes. She knew. Their

love seemed overwhelming, filling the room and Rapunzel's heart.

Flynn too, felt overcome with emotion as he stood back and watched. Rapunzel, with her emerald-green eyes, looked exactly like her beautiful mother.

Weeping with joy, the King and Queen knew, just as Rapunzel did. Their daughter, their precious child, had come home at last.

And after that? They all lived happily ever after.